Goodnight
Bear

WaterMark, Inc.

WaterMark, Inc.

Text © 2004 Hollins University
Illustrations © 2004 Sweetwater Press
Published in cooperation with Sweetwater Press
Produced by Cliff Road Books

Printed and bound in Italy
Book design by Miles Parsons

ISBN 1-88207-760-1

Goodnight Bear

Margaret Wise Brown
Illustrated by Beth Foster Wiggins

**A little bear one summer night
Flew out of the window**

And out of sight
One summer night.

He flew away to a cloudy sky
Above the world

Away up high
Where huge clouds go sailing by

**Among the stars
Where no birds fly.**

And there on a cloud the bear would lie

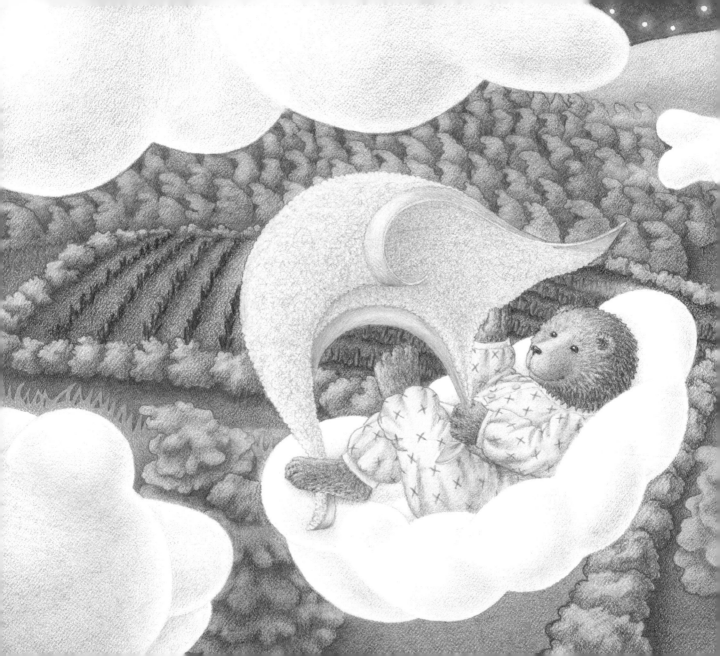

Sailing all over the windy sky

Until he woke up to a summer day

And found he had dreamed the night away.